This edition published by Parragon Books Ltd in 2014 and distributed by

Parragon Inc.
440 Park Avenue South, 13th Floor
New York, NY 10016
www.parragon.com

ISBN 978-1-4723-6724-2

Printed in China

Heidi

Based on the original
story by Johanna Spyri

*Illustrated by
Marta Belo and
Leonor Feijó*

PaRragon

Bath · New York · Cologne · Melbourne · Delhi
Hong Kong · Shenzhen · Singapore · Amsterdam

From the village of Mayenfeld, a footpath winds to the foot of the mountains and then upward. One clear, sunny morning in June, two figures were seen walking up it: one, a teenage girl named Dete, the other, a child of about four years old named Heidi. It took them a good hour to walk from Mayenfeld to the village of Dorfli, and it was another hour before they reached Heidi's grandfather's hut.

The hut stood high on the mountainside in full sunshine, with a view of the whole valley beneath. Grandfather had put up a seat outside, and here he was sitting, quietly looking out, when the pair approached. Heidi went straight up to the old man and said, "Good evening, Grandfather."

"What is the meaning of this?" he asked gruffly, giving the child an abrupt shake of the hand and scrutinizing her. Heidi stared at him in return, unable to take her eyes off his long beard and the thick eyebrows that grew together over his nose and looked just like a bush.

"I wish you good day, Uncle," said Dete. "I have brought Heidi, your granddaughter, whom you have not seen since she was a baby. She is to live with you now. I have done my duty looking after her since her mother died, and now it is time for you to do yours."

"That's it, is it?" said the old man. "And what should I do with her when she misses you?"

"That's your business," said Dete, turning on her heel and starting on the path back down the mountain. She felt uneasy about leaving the child with him, so was more rude than she had intended. Still, she told herself, she had no choice. She had a new job in the city of Frankfurt and could not look after Heidi anymore.

So Heidi was left high on a mountain with Grandfather, an old man whom she did not know, and who did not know her.

Grandfather remained seated outside his hut, staring at the ground and smoking his pipe. Heidi explored the goat shed and stared, entranced, at three tall fir trees whose top branches swayed and roared as the breeze blew through them. She then placed herself in front of Grandfather.

"What do you want?" he asked.

"I want to see inside the house," said Heidi.

"Come, then!" he said gruffly.

There was just one large room on the ground floor, with a table, a chair, a bed, a fireplace, and a large cupboard where Grandfather kept both his food and his clothes.

"Where am I to sleep?" asked Heidi.

"Wherever you like," he answered.

So Heidi explored further and found a ladder up to the hayloft. There was a large heap of fresh, sweet-smelling hay on the floor and a round window, through which she could see straight down the valley.

"I shall sleep here," she called down to him. "It's lovely. Come and see!"

"Oh, I know all about it," he called back, unable to stop himself from smiling.

While Heidi made up her bed, Grandfather found bread and cheese for them both and toasted it over a cozy fire.

After dinner, Heidi went to bed, calling down, "I like it here, Grandfather!"

Not long after, Grandfather also went to bed. The wind grew so strong during the night that the hut trembled, and the old beams groaned and creaked. Around midnight, the old man got up. "The child will be frightened," he murmured, half aloud. He climbed the ladder and went to stand by her side. Moonlight was falling through the round window straight onto Heidi's bed.

She lay under the covers, her cheeks rosy with sleep, her head peacefully resting on her little round arm, and with a happy expression on her face. The old man stood looking down on her until the moon disappeared behind the clouds and he could see no more. Then he went back to bed.

Heidi awoke early the next morning. The sun was shining through the round window, making everything in the loft golden. She climbed down the ladder quickly and ran to the door. Outside, a young goatherd, Peter, was standing with his flock, and Grandfather was bringing his own goats, Little Swan and Little Bear, out of the shed to join them.

"Do you want to go with them onto the mountain?" Grandfather asked Heidi. Nothing could have pleased Heidi better, and she jumped for joy in answer. Grandfather charged Peter with keeping her safe all day, and gave him large pieces of bread and cheese for her lunch. Peter opened his eyes wide, for Heidi's lunch was twice the size of his own. Then they were off.

Heidi was enchanted by the mountain: the bright sunshine, the green slopes, and all the little blue and yellow flowers. She ran here and there, as lively as the goats themselves, and shouted with delight. Peter had to follow, whistling, calling, and gesturing with his stick to get the runaways together again.

At lunchtime, Heidi offered to share her food with Peter. At first, he could not believe she was being so kind, but, after a minute's hesitation, he thanked her and took it gratefully.

Later in the day, one of the goats nearly fell down a sheer cliff face, and Peter only just managed to save her. He was frightened and angry, and was about to hit her with his stick, when Heidi cried, "No, Peter, you must not hit her. You have no right to touch her!" Peter looked with surprise at the commanding little figure with flashing, dark eyes. "Well, I will let her off, if you will give me some more of your cheese tomorrow," he said crossly.

"You shall have it all, tomorrow and every day," replied Heidi. "And bread, too. But you must promise not to hit any of the goats."

The bargain was agreed. Heidi was so excited about the mountain and her new life that she chattered all the way back to Grandfather's hut.

Heidi became so strong and healthy living on the mountain that nothing ever ailed her. She was happy, too, as free and light-hearted as a bird.

Winter came, and snow covered the mountain. One clear day, Grandfather got out his sleigh and took Heidi to visit Peter's grandmother, with whom Peter lived, a little way down the mountain. Grandfather left Heidi at Peter's cottage, saying that he would return later.

Peter's cottage was very different to Grandfather's. It was old, shabby, and dark, with only two tiny narrow rooms and no bright hayloft above. Heidi introduced herself to Peter's grandmother, an old woman bent with age, then looked around. One of the shutters was flapping in the breeze, filling the tiny room with banging. "Your shutter needs mending," remarked Heidi.

"Yes," said the old woman. "I am not able to see it, but I can hear its sound. The house is falling apart—it worries me so. But there is no one to mend it. Peter doesn't know how."

"Why can't you see it?" asked Heidi.

"Alas, child, I can see nothing. It is always dark for me now."

At this, Heidi started crying. "Can no one make it light for you again?" she sobbed.

"It's all right, child. Your company is doing wonders for me," the old woman said comfortingly. "Come and talk to me. Peter is always out with the goats, so I rarely hear another human voice during the day."

Heidi dried her tears and began to talk about her life on the mountain. "Grandfather will mend your house," she promised.

"I feel the darkness much less when you are with me, Heidi," said the blind grandmother.

When Grandfather collected Heidi, she told him about the grandmother's worries. "We must mend the shutter, and other things, too," she said. She looked up at him in such trustful confidence that, after a moment, he said, "Yes, Heidi, we will do that; we can mend the shutter, if nothing else." And the next day, he was as good as his word.

The seasons rolled on. Heidi learned all kinds of useful things from Grandfather, such as how to look after the goats, but she never went to school. Grandfather wanted her to grow up happy on the mountain; it was dangerous for a young child to travel down to the village school through winter winds, snow, and storms, and he had no intention of moving. Because of his gruff nature, and because he preferred living alone, he did not get along with the villagers.

One day, when Heidi was eight, Dete came to visit again. She said she had always intended to take the child back to live with her, for she well understood that Heidi must be very much in Grandfather's way. And now she had somewhere to take her. Some relatives of the family she worked for had a young daughter, an invalid in a wheelchair, who was lonely. Dete had thought at once of Heidi. She would get an education, Dete said, and who knows what other good fortune might come to her in the future in the big city of Frankfurt?

When Grandfather refused to listen to her idea, Dete was furious.

"The child knows nothing, and you will not let her learn! When there is such a good opportunity for her as this, only a person who cares for nobody and never wishes good to anyone would think of not jumping at it. You must let her go!"

"Be silent!" thundered Grandfather, his eyes flashing with anger. "Go away and never let me see you again!" And with that he strode out of the hut.

Heidi did not want to leave, but Dete convinced her that Grandfather was angry at both of them and didn't want to see her again. "The city is so nice," she said, "with lots of things to see, and if you don't like it, you can come back again when Grandfather is in a better mood."

Dete bundled Heidi down the mountain, not even allowing her time to say goodbye to the blind grandmother.

After a long day of traveling, Heidi and Dete arrived in the city and went to the house that was to be Heidi's new home. Clara, the young girl, was lying on a couch waiting for them, and Miss Rottenmeier, the housekeeper who looked after her, was sitting with her. Miss Rottenmeier did not seem pleased to see Heidi and, when she discovered that the girl was only eight years old and could not read, she was furious.

"She is completely inappropriate," she cried angrily. "How can she share school lessons when she cannot read? And Clara is four years older than her. How can she be a proper companion?"

Dete would not be put off, however, and rushed out of the house, leaving Heidi there.

Clara started to tell Heidi about the lessons, about her teacher, who was kind and would surely help Heidi to learn to read, and about how, during the classes, Miss Rottenmeier tried to hide her yawns by covering her face with her handkerchief. "Lessons will be fun now that you are here," she said, and Heidi cheered up slightly.

There were lots of rules to learn in Heidi's new home—about getting up and going to bed, shutting the doors, keeping everything tidy. And when lessons started, she found it impossible to learn the alphabet, though the teacher tried all the ways he could think of to help her. But she and Clara were becoming good friends.

After a week in the city, though, Heidi was homesick for the mountain. She hoped that she would be able to see it from one of the high windows, but all that she could see were the stony streets. Dete had said that she could go home if she didn't like it in the city, but Miss Rottenmeier said she was ungrateful to want such a thing, when she had the best of everything living with Clara. Heidi was miserable. Her only hope was that, when Clara's father came home from working away, he would let her go.

Clara's father, Mr. Sesemann, arrived late one afternoon. He greeted his daughter affectionately and then held out his hand to Heidi.

"And this must be our little visitor!" he said kindly.

"Yes, Father," said Clara. "Time has passed much more quickly since Heidi has been here, because something fresh happens every day, when it used to be so dull. And we are becoming good friends."

This convinced Mr. Sesemann that Heidi should stay with them.

Soon afterward, Clara's grandmother came to visit. There was something so very kind and warmhearted about Grandmamma that Heidi felt completely at ease. She had such beautiful white hair and two long ties that hung down from her cap and waved gently about her face every time she moved.

Grandmamma wanted to help Heidi learn to read. She showed her a pretty picture book, thinking Heidi might like it. Heidi gazed with open-eyed delight at the beautiful pictures, then, all of a sudden, as Grandmamma turned over the page, she burst into sobs. The picture showed a green field full of sheep and a shepherd looking after them. "Don't cry, dear child," said Grandmamma. "The picture has reminded you of something. But, see, there is a beautiful story to the picture that I will tell you. Dry your eyes, and we will learn to read it together."

Heidi and Grandmamma became very fond of each other and, with the lady's encouragement, Heidi was soon reading very well. But she could not tell Grandmamma how homesick she was. Sadness weighed on her heart: she could not eat; she grew pale and lay awake at night, thinking of home, or weeping quietly so that no one might hear her. Then, one night, Mr. Sesemann found Heidi sleepwalking and called in the doctor to advise what was to be done. Heidi admitted her homesickness to the kindly doctor, and it was clear what must happen. Heidi would only be cured if she went home.

Heidi was in such a state of excitement when she learned that she was going home that she hardly knew if she was awake or dreaming. Her face glowed rosy with delight as she ran to say goodbye to Clara. Clara was very upset about Heidi leaving, but Mr. Sesemann promised that he would take Clara to Switzerland to visit Heidi the next summer. Then it was time to leave. Mr. Sesemann wished Heidi a happy journey; she thanked him for all his kindness, and the carriage took her away.

After a long journey, first by train and then by horse and cart, Heidi found herself back in Dorfli. She trembled with excitement, for she knew every tree and rock, and the jagged peak of the mountain looking down on her was like an old friend. Up the steep path she went and at last caught sight of the grandmother's house. She ran faster and faster, her heart beating louder and louder, until she was inside.

"It is I, Grandmother," she cried, and she flung herself on her knees beside the old woman and clung to her.

The grandmother stroked Heidi's hair and cried tears of joy.

"I am never going away again," said the girl, "and I shall come every day to see you."

She bade the grandmother goodbye and continued up to Grandfather's hut. When she saw him, Heidi rushed up to him and flung her arms around his neck. He had missed her so much that he started to cry.

"So you have come back to me, Heidi," he said. "Did they send you away?"

"Oh no, Grandfather," said Heidi, "but I longed to be home again with you. I used to think I should die, for I felt as if I could not breathe in the city."

There was a shrill whistle, and Peter appeared with his goats. He beamed with pleasure when he saw Heidi and took the hand that she was holding out in greeting.

Heidi was home at last.

The next day, Heidi went down the mountain to visit the grandmother, as she had promised. The grandmother heard her steps approaching and greeted her as she entered. Then she took hold of Heidi's hand and held it tightly in her own, for she still seemed to fear that the child might be torn from her again.

Heidi caught sight of a hymn book, and a happy idea came to her.

"I can read now," she said. "Would you like me to read you a hymn?"

"Oh, yes," said the grandmother, surprised and delighted. Heidi took the book down from its shelf, where it had lain untouched for years. Then she turned the pages until she found a good one.

"Here is one about the sun, Grandmother. I will read you this."

The grandmother sat with folded hands and a look of indescribable joy on her face as Heidi read. "That brings light to the heart!" she said. "What comfort you have brought me!"

"I will come again tomorrow and read to you every day," Heidi promised.

When she got home to Grandfather again, Heidi told him how happy the grandmother was to have hymns read to her. "Everything is happier now than it has ever been in our lives before!" she cried. "If I had come home sooner, as I wanted to, I would not have known how to read, and so I would not have been able to bring comfort to the grandmother in the way I now can. Everything happens for the best, in its own good time. Isn't that right, Grandfather?"

Heidi's words played on the old man's mind. He realized that he had been wrong to live so far from Dorfli, so isolated from everyone. He also now knew how much he loved Heidi, and how she deserved to live near other children and go to school like them. So he vowed that, when the first snow of winter began to fall, he would close up the hut and take Heidi down to live in Dorfli.

Heidi was delighted with her new home in Dorfli, and enjoyed her first days at school, too. On the fourth morning in the village, she said to Grandfather, "I must go up the mountain to see the grandmother. It makes her so happy when I read to her."

But Grandfather would not let her go. "The snow is too deep and still falling. You must wait till it freezes, and then you will be able to walk over the hard snow."

When Heidi next visited the grandmother, she found her in bed, trying to keep warm. Heidi read to her, one hymn after another, and a smile of peace spread over the old woman's face.

"Thank you for reading, my child," she said. "No one knows what it is to lie here alone day after day, in silence and darkness, without hearing a voice or seeing a ray of light. When you come and read those words to me, I am comforted."

"If I could read to Grandmother every day," Heidi thought to herself, "then I should go on making her better. But I cannot." Suddenly, an idea struck her. Peter must learn to read, so that he could read to the grandmother, too!

When she told Peter her idea, he shrugged. "I've tried to learn, but I've never been able to," he said, shamefacedly. "That's why I hate school."

"Well, I will teach you," said Heidi, "and we will start now."

She pulled out a book that Clara had given her and started reading each sentence aloud to him. He then repeated it back to her.

"Good," said Heidi. "If I teach you every evening, and you learn as you have today, you will soon know all your letters."

And so the winter went by, and Peter made real progress, until, one evening, he was finally able to read to his grandmother. His reading was not perfect—in fact, he left out words he found too long or difficult, and the grandmother sometimes lost the sense of the hymn—but his intentions were always good.

Spring came again. The full, fresh streams were flowing down into the valley and clear, warm sunshine lay on the green slopes. After spending the winter in Dorfli, Heidi and Grandfather were back on the mountain for the summer.

One hot day at the end of June, a strange-looking procession came up the mountain: a girl being carried carefully by a servant, a stately-looking lady on a horse, an empty wheelchair being pushed by another servant, and, finally, a porter carrying a huge bundle of cloaks and shawls. It was Clara and her grandmother, finally coming to visit.

Heidi and Grandfather rushed forward to meet them, and the two children hugged each other. Grandmamma embraced Heidi, then turned to Grandfather and greeted him warmly. They had heard so much about each other from Heidi in the past that it was as if they were old friends.

Grandfather lifted Clara and sat her gently in her wheelchair, as carefully as if he had looked after her all his life. Then Heidi wheeled her around to see the fir trees, the goat shed, and the flowers on the mountain slopes. The wheelchair was too wide to go through the hut's door, so Grandfather lifted Clara again and carried her around to see inside, even taking her up the ladder to Heidi's hayloft bedroom.

Clara was entranced with everything, and her face glowed with excitement at it all. Seeing this, Grandfather said to Grandmamma, "Madam, if you were willing, your granddaughter might stay up here for a little, rather than go back down to Dorfli with you. I am sure she will grow stronger if she stays. We will take great care of her."

"My dear sir," replied Grandmamma, "you give words to the thought that was in my own mind." Then she took his hand and gave it a long and grateful shake. Clara and Heidi were overjoyed.

So Clara stayed with Heidi and Grandfather, and slept with Heidi in the hayloft bedroom, lit at night by the moon and stars.

Clara loved life on the mountain, and Heidi was the best of companions. Grandfather helped Clara to stand a little each day, and, though it hurt her, she made the effort in order to please him.

Every day, Peter asked Heidi to come out to the mountain with him, but she could not leave Clara. Peter was jealous of Heidi's new friend, and one day his anger boiled over. Seeing the wheelchair outside Grandfather's hut, he pushed it down a steep slope. It fell and smashed on the rocks below. "Now Clara will have to leave," he thought.

Indeed, it did seem impossible for Clara to stay. But Heidi had such confidence and happiness in her heart that she believed *anything* was possible. And then, the impossible *did* happen.

Heidi had recently discovered a distant meadow of flowers, gold, deep blue, and sweet-smelling red-brown. She longed for her friend to see it, too. Grandfather was not there, and Heidi could not carry Clara alone, so she called Peter to help. Peter was still cross, but he also felt guilty about the wheelchair, so he agreed. Leaning on him, and with Heidi's encouragement, Clara took first one step, then another—and, finally, she walked to see the flowers!

After that, Clara walked every day. When Grandmamma and Mr. Sesemann came to take her back to the city, they were amazed, and their gratefulness to Heidi and Grandfather knew no end. They promised that Clara would come back the following year.

And what of Peter? Grandfather guessed that he had destroyed the chair and thought the boy should be punished. But Grandmamma kindly said to Peter, "What you did was wrong. But if you had not done it, Clara would not have had to make the effort to walk."

Heidi's heart was filled with joy. She was at home with those whom she loved most and who loved her.

"Everything always turns out for the best," she told herself and smiled.